D1315402

THE IBIS AND THE EGRET

Roy Owen

THE IBIS AND THE EGRET

illustrated by Robert Sabuda

PHILOMEL BOOKS
NEW YORK

Philomel Books, a division of The Putnam & Grosset Group,

200 Madison Avenue, New York, NY 10016. Published simultaneously in Canada.

Printed in Hong Kong by South China Printing Co. (1988) Ltd.

Book design by Gunta Alexander.   The text is set in Tiepolo.

Library of Congress Cataloging-in-Publication Data   Owen, Roy.   The ibis and the egret
/ Roy Owen; illustrated by Robert Sabuda. p.   cm.   Summary: The ibis and the egret
celebrate each of the four seasons by finding things they like about it.   [I. Seasons—Fiction.
2. Ibis—Fiction. 3. Herons—Fiction.]   I. Sabuda, Robert, ill.   II. Title.   PZ7.09715Ib
1993   [E]—dc20   92-26220   CIP   AC   ISBN 0-399-22504-8

1   3   5   7   9   10   8   6   4   2

First Impression

To Bryn and Hadley — R.O.

In memory of Wesley Smith, who made us laugh — R.S.

I think spring is my favorite season," said the Ibis to the Egret one fine spring day.

"With the marsh turning green and the wind on the water,

and the land birds singing and the ducks heading north,

and the new blue crabs swimming on the rising spring tide,
don't you think spring is your favorite time?"
"Yes," said the Egret, "I, too, like the springtime,
for all of those reasons, and more of my own.
I know of no season I like better than spring."

"I think summer is my favorite season,"
said the Ibis to the Egret one fine summer's day.
"With long lines of pelicans skimming the wave tops
and small groups of sandpipers piping the shore,
with the marsh in full green and the sun bright and warm,

creeks filled with shrimp on the incoming tide
and the cry of the marsh hen in the
long summer evening,

don't you think summer is your favorite time?"
"Yes," said the Egret, "I, too, like the summer.
I know of no season I like better than this."

"I think autumn is my favorite season,"
said the Ibis to the Egret one crisp autumn day.
"With the light on the water
and the marsh turning golden,

with the ducks heading south
and the world growing still,
don't you think autumn is your favorite time?"
"Yes," said the Egret, "I, too, like the autumn.
I know of no season I like better than this."

"I think winter is my favorite season,"
said the Ibis to the Egret one cold winter's day.
"With the gray of the sky and the gray of the water,
and the gray of the marsh all flooded and quiet,

the white of our wings in the quiet gray stillness
is all that is moving, is all I can see.
Don't you think winter is truly our season,

don't you think winter's your favorite time?"
"Yes," said the Egret, "I, too, like the winter.
With each year that passes, I like winter more."

"Why is it, Egret, that you and I stay here?
We've seen all the seasons.
Why don't we fly on?

The ducks and the land birds fly north in the springtime,

the crabs and the shrimp, they come and they go.

The tides ebb and flow, the marsh changes colors, everything changes except you and me."

"Be still, dear Ibis. Be quiet and still.
And watch while the seasons bring new life our way.

For the ducks and the land birds, life is all springtime.
Crabs never know winter. All the sun knows is day.

But you and I, Ibis, can see more than others.
So be still, dear Ibis, be quiet and still."